"Antonio!" Salem shouted as he raced to help his friend.

With his front paws he pushed the little dog out of the way just as the tires of the large white truck squealed and skidded. The wheels smoked, and the smell of burned rubber filled the air.

Antonio tumbled against the curb and landed in a heap. He stretched out his legs and started to stand. "Oh Salem, *mi amigo*," he said in a rush, "you saved my life!"

"It was nothing," Salem said. Then he shrugged. "Well, okay, it was extremely brave and self-sacrificing of me. However, leaders are required to be brave and self—"

But he never got to finish his sentence. For just as Antonio shouted, "Look out!" a huge net came crashing down on top of Salem.

Sabrina, the Teenage Witch™
Salem's Tails™

#1 CAT TV
   Salem Goes to Rome
#2 Teacher's Pet
#3 You're History!
#4 The King of Cats
#5 Dog Day Afternoon
#6 Psychic Kitty
#7 Cat by the Tail
#8 Feline Felon

Available from MINSTREL Books

Sabrina The Teenage Witch

Salem's Tails™

FELINE FELON

Nancy Holder

Based on Characters Appearing in Archie Comics

**And based upon the television series
Sabrina, The Teenage Witch
Created for television by Nell Scovell
Developed for television by Jonathan Schmock**

Illustrated by Mark Dubowski

A MINSTREL® BOOK

Published by POCKET BOOKS
New York   London   Toronto   Sydney   Tokyo   Singapore

A MINSTREL PAPERBACK *Original*

A Minstrel Book published by
POCKET BOOKS, a division of Simon & Schuster Inc.
1230 Avenue of the Americas, New York, NY 10020

ISBN: 0-671-02384-5

First Minstrel Books printing September 1999

10 9 8 7 6 5 4 3 2 1

Printed in the U.S.A.

For the little ones:
Olivia Shiffman-Yee, Grace Beck, Sarah Wilcox,
Melody and Mallory Nierman, Duncan Klug, and
Belle and Clarissa Holder, of course!

And for Rebecca Morhaim, too,
even if she's not very little anymore.

I urge you to accept me as your ruler. . . .
                                    —*Salem*

Chapter 1

"Sabrina, can't you dust any faster than that?" demanded Salem, the big black cat that lived with the teenage witch. A large American shorthair, he was no ordinary feline. He had once been a powerful warlock who had tried to take over the world. When the Witches' Council found out what he was up to, they put a stop to his plans and turned him into a cat for one hundred years. The only thing remaining of his old life was his ability to talk. But he never let mortals hear him. He reserved his conversations for witches.

At the moment, he was curled up on the sofa in the living room of the Victorian house he and Sabrina shared with Sabrina's aunts. They were also witches, and their names were Hilda and Zelda Spellman. They had invited Sabrina to move in with them a few years before in order to teach her to use her magic powers responsibly. They sure didn't want her to end up like Salem!

"Salem, you should be grateful I'm helping you," Sabrina said. She waved her pointer finger back and forth, back and forth. Across the room a magic feather duster copied Sabrina's movements. It was busily dusting the TV, which probably didn't need very much dusting. Salem loved to watch TV. Especially soap operas. And he was very fond of *Those Amazing Animals.*

"In fact," Sabrina continued with a wave of her blond hair, "you should be glad I'm helping you at all! You know, the Witches' Council isn't all that thrilled about this reunion you've cooked up."

Salem sniffed. "Even thwarted world leaders need to have some fun now and then."

Salem had decided to host a reunion weekend for all the witches and war-locks who had been turned into animals as punishment for trying take over the Mortal Realm at one time or another. It was surprising how many there were.

Ambition. It makes you . . . ambi-tious, Salem thought.

Salem was both excited and nervous about the weekend. *I want everything*

3

to be perfect! He had even taken dance lessons. He could do the cha-cha!

"We didn't buy enough tuna puffs for the get-acquainted party," he said suddenly, fretting. "And the dried squid hasn't shown up yet! I'll never have everything ready in time!"

"Salem, we're witches," Sabrina reminded him. "It'll only take a little while to get ready."

"Time to panic!" Salem cried.

Then the doorbell rang.

"Time to answer the door!" he shouted.

"Okay, okay, calm down," Sabrina urged.

Salem trotted behind her as she opened the door. The first thing he saw was a tall man carrying a suitcase.

"Amigo!" the man cried, bending down to shake Salem's paw. "Long time no see."

4

"Yes, I mean *sí,*" Salem replied. He was happy enough to greet the man, whose name was Emilio Gutierrez. He was a warlock from Mexico City, who also happened to have friends in show business. That was one reason Salem was always glad to see him.

But then the main reason Salem was happy to see Emilio stuck his head around Emilio's leg. With a happy cry, a small, hairless dog with enormous black eyes skittered on the hardwood floor toward Salem.

"My leader!" the little dog shouted.

He was Antonio, once also a powerful warlock. He had fought alongside his commander-in-chief, Salem, in his bid for world domination. And like Salem, he had been punished. Now he was a Chihuahua. Privately, Salem thought Antonio's punishment—to be a *dog*—was even worse than his own. *Also, being hairless must be strange.* As a warlock, Antonio had worn a long, dark beard, and his eyebrows had been very thick and bushy.

"Come in, come in!" Salem said warmly. "The house is a mess, but please make yourselves at home. As they say in Mexico, *mi casa es su casa.*"

"If that is indeed true, we would be most grateful," Antonio said. "It seems that our reservations at the Hartbreak Hotel have been misplaced, and we need a place to stay."

"Just until the confusion is sorted out," Emilio added. "If your family does not mind?" He smiled at Salem and then at Sabrina.

"Oh, we'd just love it if you stayed for days and days and days," Salem said, delighted. "Right, Sabrina?"

"Oh, yes, right," she said po— as she led the way into the living room.

Salem plopped down on the couch, and Antonio hopped up beside him. He sprawled out with his head on a pillow.

Emilio set down his suitcase and gestured to the living room. "You have a lovely home," he said. "Just as Salem described it." He smiled at Sabrina, who was actually rather charmed.

Then he added, "This room will be perfect for salsa dancing. You do dance, do you not?" he asked Sabrina.

"Uh, sure. Maybe not as well as Salem. I've never taken lessons."

"Oh, I would be glad to teach you." He moved his shoulders and hips. "It's very simple."

"It doesn't look simple," Sabrina confessed. "But I'd be glad to give it a try."

Salem was so happy he began knead-

...he couch cushion. "Oh, this was such a great idea," he said. "Can't you just feel it, Sabrina? Adventure is in the air."

"Woof, woof," Antonio yipped. "It's just like the old days, Salem!"

"Gee, ya think?" Salem asked him, his eyes gleaming. "Maybe we could try to take over the *animal* kingdom. . . ."

"Stick to the cha-cha," Sabrina said darkly. "You two don't want to get into any more trouble."

Salem blinked innocently at her. "Relax, Sabrina, we're just kidding. Besides," he added, flicking his tail, "how much trouble could we get in?"

Chapter 2

While Sabrina showed Emilio around the house, Salem and Antonio remembered old times. "You were a wonderful leader," Antonio told Salem. "Always planning for the next big battle. Remember when Hans and Fritz accidentally locked themselves inside that castle? It was genius how you got those enemy soldiers to lower the drawbridge."

"No one can resist free cookies," Salem said proudly. He and Antonio had disguised themselves in the green uniforms of the Girl Scouts. The two had told the soldiers that someone had sent them an enormous order of cookies as a gift. The soldiers hadn't hesitated for one minute to let them inside the castle.

The rest was part of Salem's glorious past.

Just then Emilio and Sabrina came up to them. He was smiling broadly. "So, *amigos*, how's it going? Antonio, shall I go ahead and cast the spell?"

"*Sí, sí!*" Antonio said enthusiastically. He said to Salem, "Emilio always casts an 'Animals Walk, Animals Talk' spell whenever we travel together." He raised and lowered his eyebrows. "It makes it a lot easier for me to meet girls."

"I completely understand," Salem said, nodding. Only witchy familiars and fallen world leaders could talk. The animals in the Mortal Realm only barked, cooed, and meowed, as a rule.

"Emilio!" Sabrina's Aunt Zelda called from the front door. "How lovely to see you. Antonio, *bienvenidos*."

"Ah, Señorita Zelda, you're as lovely as always," Emilio said. "And your home is so beautiful. As pretty as your niece." He gestured to Sabrina, who stood beside him.

"Oh, you say all the right things." Zelda grinned at him.

"I was about to cast a spell for Antonio," he said. "May I use your kitchen?"

"Of course. And I'd be glad to assist you."

"*Muchas gracias.*"

"Where's Aunt Hilda?" Sabrina asked.

"She's shopping for party refreshments," Zelda said. "She should be home any minute."

The two witches and the warlock headed for the kitchen.

"As soon as they're finished," Salem said, rubbing his paws together in anticipation, "we'll go prowling for some lovely ladies."

Antonio's huge brown eyes glittered. "I thought your people didn't like you to leave the house," he whispered.

"Oh, them?" Salem rolled his eyes. "They're overly cautious. Always expecting me to get into mischief. Or at the very least, to cause some." He winked at Antonio. "A cat can dream, can't he?"

"So can a dog," Antonio said. He trotted over to the doorway, and they both peered into the kitchen. Emilio was mixing something on the stove and chanting.

Antonio added, "And it won't be long now before I can introduce myself to some pretty little poodle. I'm a fool for poodles."

"I'm going for a longhair," Salem declared. "They shed, but boy, can they root through trash cans."

"Listen," Antonio said, laying a paw over Salem's. "I almost forgot. Christophe is already in town. He's staying at the same hotel as we are. Or rather, as we are supposed to be. The Hartbreak."

"Excellent!" Salem cried. Christophe and Antonio had been Salem's two most trusted soldiers in his attempt to take over the world. "Let's surprise him with a visit!"

"*Sí, sí,*" Antonio said eagerly. "As soon as Emilio is finished with the spell, we'll pick up Christophe and the three of us will go searching for romance and adventure!"

"I'm in," Salem replied. "Let's go now!"

Antonio's black claws clattered on the

13

floor as the two friends skidded toward the front door. Then Antonio turned to Salem and said, *"Uno minuto, amigo. Don't you need to tell the Spellman ladies where you're going?"*

Salem was embarrassed by Antonio's question. After all, the last time they had seen each other, Salem was Antonio's fearless leader. Back then, no one dared to tell Salem Saberhagen what to do! Well, maybe except for his mother.

But that was different. He wasn't about to humiliate himself by asking permission to leave the house.

"No way, *amigo*," Salem announced. "I may be a cat now, but I'm nobody's house pet! I come and go as I please. Always have. Always will."

Antonio's face lit up with awe. "You were always the brave one, Salem," he said in a hushed voice. "That's why we followed you. That, and the terrific refreshments that Hilda provided."

"No one's ever pointed up spicier nachos," Salem agreed, recalling the good old days. "She said she'd make some for the party."

"Oh, how wonderful! You know, life as a Chihuahua has turned out to be pretty good, so far."

"And we're about to make it even better," Salem announced.

Just then the front door opened. Sabrina's Aunt Hilda called out, "Hello! Anybody home? I have about a hundred pounds of tortilla chips in the car that I need help unloading."

"Later, toots," Salem murmured as he and Antonio darted around her legs, out of the house, and headed for adventure.

Chapter 3

An hour passed. Then two. The streetlights of Westbridge blinked on as the sun set. Then the moon rose, casting golden beams down on one very tired Chihuahua and one very confused and lost black American shorthair cat.

"Salem, I'm so sorry," Antonio said. "I'm completely confused. I thought I knew the way to the hotel from your house, but clearly, I made a mistake. We've walked all over Westbridge, but we have never come across the Hart-break Hotel."

Salem grunted. He was very hungry and his foot pads were blistered. "Well, I can't think of anywhere else to look. We've gone up and down every alley, crossed every single busy intersection, and trotted around and around all the traffic circles I can think of."

Antonio hung his head. "And to make matters worse, not a single fur-covered *amigo* can give us correct directions when we ask for them."

"And women wonder why we never ask for directions," Salem groused. He sighed. "Let's face it, Antonio. We have the hotel name wrong, or the street, or something. I say we find a pay phone and call a cab."

Antonio looked shocked. "A cat and a dog, calling a taxi?"

17

Salem shrugged. "It would probably work in a Saturday morning animated series. Listen, Antonio." His stomach growled. "No, not to my stomach," he said, making a face as the little hairless dog moved toward his tummy. "I just want to go home. Sure, the Spellmans and Emilio are going to yell at us, but I don't care anymore."

"Why would they yell? You said you can come and go as you please," Antonio protested. "If I had realized we had broken a house rule—"

"What?" Salem challenged him.

Antonio grinned. "Then I would have laughed when we dodged around Hilda," he admitted. "Once a rebel, always a rebel, eh, Salem?"

Salem chuckled. "They'll never housebreak you!" he said. They high-fived each other.

Together, they crossed another four-lane road, dodging enormous trucks, speeding cars, and noisy motorcycles that veered in and out of traffic.

Then Salem pointed to a pay phone booth on the opposite corner.

"Here's what we'll do," he suggested. "You prop yourself up on your hind legs, and I'll climb up behind your neck, and then I'll chin up on the little ledge and . . ."

He sighed in frustration. "What am I talking about? We don't have any money."

"We can call collect," Antonio said.

"No, we can't. Zelda put a Salem Alert spell on our phone because my last bill was so high. It will refuse to put any call I make through if I don't pay for it in advance."

"911 is free," Antonio suggested.

19

Salem shook his head. "The fine for misusing it is huge. We'd be paying it off for the rest of our lives."

"Oh." Antonio looked disappointed. He sat at the curb, shivering. "I'm cold, Salem," he admitted. "I'm not used to the weather up here. And I'm hairless, as you may have noticed. I have no fur coat to warm me."

Salem sat down beside him. "Our easy lives as pets have made us soft, Antonio," he said sadly. "I live in a climate-controlled house just bulging with sweaters and other soft things to lie on. And to shred . . ." he added dreamily. "Things were different when we were soldiers. I remember freezing nights when we could see our breath. We huddled around tiny campfires as we planned our next assault on the Mortal Realm!"

"*Sí,*" Antonio murmured. "Hilda always made hot chocolate on those nights. With the little marshmallows."

"With the little marshmallows," Salem echoed. "I had so much in my paws, Antonio. I was almost king of the world. And now I can't even phone home."

Then suddenly Antonio's ears pricked up. He gave a little yip and got to his paws.

"Salem, look! In the rain gutter across the street!"

Salem squinted. His heart leaped. There was something shiny across the street. *A coin?* Salem craned his neck. *Yes! Enough to phone for a cab!* Or even to break down and call one of the Spellmans to pick them up.

"Yes!" Salem cried happily. "All right, Antonio. Let's go get that money."

"*Dinero,* in my language." Antonio nodded with excitement. "As soon as the light changes, *sí?* One, two, *three!*"

21

Antonio hopped down from the curb. Salem hesitated. Like a good city cat, he always looked left, right, then left again before he crossed.

Left . . .

"Come on, come on!" Antonio urged, glancing at Salem over his shoulder.

"I'm coming," Salem said.

Right . . .

As he turned his head again, he caught his breath and shouted, "Antonio! Look out!"

A large white truck was racing straight for Antonio. In another minute it would surely hit him!

Chapter 4

"Antonio!" Salem shouted as he raced to help his friend. With his front paws he pushed the little dog out of the way just as the tires of the large white truck squealed and skidded. The wheels smoked, and the smell of burned rubber filled the air.

Antonio tumbled against the curb and landed in a heap. He stretched out his legs and started to stand. "Oh, Salem, *mi amigo,*" he said in a rush, "you saved my life!"

"It was nothing," Salem said. Then he shrugged. "Well, okay, it was extremely brave and self-sacrificing of me. However, leaders are required to be brave and self—"

But he never got to finish his sentence. For just as Antonio shouted, "Look out!" a huge net came crashing down on top of Salem.

"What is the meaning of this!" Salem sputtered, thrashing inside the net. He pawed at the trap, but only succeeded in getting more tangled up.

"Who said that?" a man shouted, looking around.

Through the crisscross pattern of the net, Salem looked up at the man. He wore an olive-green uniform, and on his shirt was a badge that read WESTBRIDGE ANIMAL CONTROL. He held on to a long pole. The opposite end of it was attached to Salem's net.

He's a dog*catcher,* Salem thought indignantly. *And excuse me very much, but I am a cat.*

"What did you snag, Jake?" another man asked. He was coming around from the other side of the truck. He was tall and red-haired, and he carried a net on a pole as well.

"I've got some kind of chubby, hairy terrier," Salem's captor—Jake—announced.

I beg your pardon, Salem thought, completely insulted. But he didn't speak this time. He wasn't supposed to let mortals know he could talk. And this was a situation he doubted he could talk himself out of anyway.

The red-haired man gestured with the

net toward Antonio. The Chihuahua was still standing beside the curb.

He's being loyal to me, Salem thought proudly. *He's standing his ground in case he can rescue me.*

"Hey, little guy," the man said. "You look pretty scared. Don't be. We won't hurt you."

"Antonio, run," Salem whispered. "I order you to *andale!*"

Antonio continued to hover beside the curb. As the redheaded man crept closer, Antonio started to whimper and tried to move. He had been hurt. He limped only a few inches before the red-haired man's net surrounded him.

"Got him!" the man said, chuckling as Antonio yipped wildly. "Take it easy, boy." He held the net with both hands. "This is one little dog that doesn't want to stop playing in traffic."

"If only they knew we were doing this for their own good," Jake said. "Then they wouldn't fight us."

"Wanna bet, *amigo?*" Antonio muttered.

"Ssh," Salem warned.

"Well, I guess that's it," Jake said with satisfaction. "It's almost quitting time. We'll take these two in and call it a day."

"Sure thing, Jake."

The red-haired man hefted the net over his shoulder. Antonio grunted but remained silent. But his large eyes told Salem exactly what he, himself, was thinking: *We're in big trouble.*

Then Salem's net went up over Jake's shoulder. It swung in a most undignified manner as the man walked back to the van, whistling to himself.

Doesn't he know there are no leash laws for cats in Westbridge? Salem

27

thought. *Cats are allowed to roam free. I have committed no crime. And Antonio is a guest in our fair town! And he's a decorated war veteran! Well, okay, a veteran fighter of my private war, and I was the one who decorated him—with lots of medals. But he should not be treated like a common criminal!*

"Here you go, big fella," Jake said as he slid open the van and opened up a wire mesh cage. He slid Salem into the cage and flipped it over, so that Salem landed on his feet. Of course he landed on his feet. Cats always did!

Jake closed and locked Salem's cage door while the other man put Antonio into the cage beside it. The red-haired man gave each door a little pat. Then Jake slid the van door shut. After a few moments the van engine roared to life.

"Oh, this is terrible," Antonio whispered to Salem.

"We've been in worse scrapes than this one," Salem reminded him. "Remember the Alamo?"

Antonio shook his head.

"That's because we weren't there," Salem said slowly. "But if we had been, we would have saved everybody. We are fierce warriors, Antonio. We've gotten out of seemingly hopeless scrapes before."

"*Sí*, but this time you're a cat, and I'm a dog. And I certainly mean no insult, Salem, but ah, er, you're a little out of shape."

"*What?*" Salem was cut to the quick. First, some mortal mistook him for a dog, and now one of his old officers was insulting him! "I just live well," he insisted.

"You always had to watch your

29

weight, even when we were starving in the trenches," Antonio reminded him.

Salem drew himself up to his full height. Unfortunately, it was not all that high. And his stomach *was* kind of noticeably bulging.

"I will lead you out of this, Antonio," Salem promised the dog. "I still have the right stuff to be a fearless leader, and I'm going to prove it."

"Good," Antonio said enthusiastically.

"I'm going to break us out of here and get us home."

"Hurray!" Antonio cried, but it came out as a yip.

"Yes, that's what I'm going to do!"

"*Bravo!*" Then Antonio hesitated and asked, "When?"

"Soon," Salem replied. "Very, very soon."

"How?"

"I'm working on that." Salem curled up on the hard wire floor and leaned his head on his paws. "I'll just rest my eyes while I run down the list of possibilities. There are a lot of details to consider. Yes, indeed."

"Salem?" Antonio called as if from far away.

But Salem didn't answer.

He was fast asleep.

Chapter 5

Salem woke up shouting, "Troops! Advance on the enemy! Attack!"

He had been dreaming again about taking over the mortal realm. It was a wonderful dream. This time he won the war and was just about to be crowned King of Every Single Thing when he suddenly woke up.

Smiling to himself, he stretched. Then he opened his eyes.

He blinked in surprise. He was in another wire cage! It was just like the one he had been locked into inside the van. It was one of several placed in a row, with more cages stacked on top. It was kind of like a cage apartment building.

What a horrible invention, he thought, shuddering.

Beyond the gate to his cage was a spotless, dark gray concrete floor. About five feet away another row of cages faced his. Several of the cages contained dogs, including a large black-and-white Dalmatian that stared curiously at Salem. Another cage held a big-eyed raccoon. Two long brown ferrets were locked up next to each other on the other side of the Dalmatian.

Beside the row of cages, in a bird cage on a pedestal, a brilliantly colored parrot squawked, "Troops! Attack! Awk!"

Salem frowned, then said, "Where am I?"

"We're in prison," Antonio said unhappily. He sat in the cage on Salem's right. His hind leg was wrapped in bandages. "They brought us in while you were still asleep."

"Asleep!" Salem cried. "I was not . . . okay, I did fall asleep," he admitted. "I'm not used to so much physical activity. What did they do to you?" He gestured at Antonio's bandages.

"I scraped my leg when you knocked me out of the way," Antonio said. "Not that I am blaming you, of course. You saved my life."

"Yes." *And I never get tired of being thanked for things like that,* Salem thought.

"The night keeper bandaged it himself," Antonio said, his eyes going soft and dreamy. "His name is Howard. He's nice, for a jailer."

"Well, I'm glad this Howard looked after you." Salem frowned. "But he must have noticed that I'm a *cat*. Why'd he lock me up?"

"He decided you must be a house cat," Antonio explained. "He thought it would be cruel to let you out."

"Cruel?" Salem was confused. "How can giving me my freedom be cruel?"

"He said you looked like you were lost," Antonio told him. "He was afraid you wouldn't make it back home in one piece."

Antonio lowered his voice. "He said it's a *jungle* out there, my friend."

"Well, it is. But not the kind of jungle we fought in during our quest for world domination," Salem said, sighing. "That one was full of trees and snakes. This one is full of cars and Doberman pinschers."

He looked around. "In the movies the prisoners always get to make one phone call. I'll just phone Sabrina and ask her to come get us."

"No phone calls for us, *amigo*," Antonio reminded him. "We're animals, remember?"

Salem flopped over on his side. "Oh, this is just great," he grumbled. "The reunion begins tomorrow. I have a thousand things to do to prepare for it, and I'm stuck in the slammer!"

"It's always hard for the new ones," said the dog across from Salem. He was a tall and muscular Dalmatian, white with lots of black spots all over his body. One of his eyes was surrounded by black, while the fur around the other one was white.

"Welcome to the dog pound," he said. "It's really not so bad. Unless you're used to something better."

"I *am*. Hey!" Salem cocked his head. "You're talking."

"It's very strange," the dog mused. "Suddenly we can all talk."

"We can all talk!" the parrot chirped.

The Dalmatian grinned at Salem. "Well, Polly just repeats everything we say. But she's always been able to do that."

"When did this happen?" Salem asked.

"Earlier today," the Dalmatian told him. "A few hours before they brought you two in."

"Salem," Antonio said quietly, "it must be from when Emilio cast the 'talking animal' spell."

"I think it's *fabuloso*," said a sultry

voice. Salem craned his neck to see through the mesh into the cage on the other side of Antonio. It was another Chihuahua. Only this one wore a sparkly jeweled collar adorned with a pastel pink bow. And from the look on Antonio's face, she was a lovely girl, for a dog.

"This is Señorita Maria Tacquito," Antonio said to Salem. "We had a long chat while you were asleep. She used to be a TV star!"

"Commercials," she drawled. "Fast food, mostly. I even had my own T-shirts." She sighed, rose, and scratched herself.

She continued, "I tried to move into films, but it didn't work out. I decided to spend some time away from Hollywood, so I came to the East Coast. And now I'm stuck in this fleabag joint!"

"We'll get you out," Antonio said. "Won't we, my fearless leader?"

All eyes turned toward Salem.

Uh-oh!

Salem was about to answer when footsteps rang on the floor. The other animals got to their paws or claws and arched their necks in the direction of a large closed door to Salem's right.

"It's Howard," the Dalmatian announced. "He's bringing our dinner."

"Awk! Polly want a cracker!" the parrot clucked.

"We'll escape as soon as possible. Right, Salem?" Antonio said urgently.

Salem's mouth began to water. *Dinner! How wonderful.* He was starving.

"Sure, Antonio. Right after we eat," he promised.

After all, he reasoned, *fearless leaders*

hatch better escape plans after a nice, big meal.

Or else they fall asleep, he added.

Howard the keeper was just about to open the door.

"Okay, listen up and listen good," Salem said to the others. "Do *not* talk around humans. You'll get into more trouble than you can imagine."

"It sounds as if you've learned that lesson the hard way," the Dalmatian said.

"Believe me, I have." Salem rolled his eyes. *The stories I could tell this group!*

"Me, too," Antonio said. "The stories I could tell you!"

"All right, then." The Dalmatian nodded. "We'll follow your example. Okay, everybody?"

"Okeydokey," the raccoon piped.

"Yessiree, Bob!" a Pekingese joined in.

"Mum's the word!" a third voice chirruped.

Before Salem could hush them, all the animals were very noisily agreeing to be quiet.

But everyone fell silent as soon as the door opened.

Howard was a young man about six feet tall, wearing a sweatshirt that read BOSTON COLLEGE and a pair of well-worn jeans. He was pushing an aluminum cart containing several metal bowls with one hand and holding a thick book with the other. He was reading the book intently.

Salem sniffed the air expectantly and murmured, "Tuna. It's what's for dinner. Oh, please, please, please."

The man put down his book and picked up a dish of food. He went to the first cage on the row facing Salem and bent down.

4 1

"Evening, Delilah," the man said to the Pekingese inside the first cage as he carefully opened the gate. "Here's your kibble."

The dog named Delilah opened her mouth, glanced at Salem, and said, "Woof." Then she dived into the bowl and started gobbling.

Hmm. So at least they feed the prisoners well around here, Salem thought eagerly.

"And here's yours, Fireplug," he said to the Dalmatian.

The man put dishes down inside all the cages on the bottom row. There was dog food for the dogs, some fruit for the raccoon, and rabbit food for the ferrets. The parrot received birdseed.

But when the man got to Salem's cage, he frowned and said, "I'm sorry, Mr. Kitty, but we don't have any cat food

today. I can give you dog food, though."
He smiled kindly. "How would you like
that?"

Yuck! Salem thought. He hunkered
down and put his chin on his front
paws.

"Why don't you try it?" Howard asked
as he opened Salem's cage. He set down
a bowl of dull brown cubes and a dish
of water. Salem paid him very little attention. The black cat was trying to see
if he could squeeze his way past the
man's arm and dart out of the cage.

He looked down at himself and
sighed. He was a little too big. *Make
that formerly well-fed.*

"I hope you enjoy it," Howard said
sincerely. Then he moved on to the
next animal.

Salem stuck a paw in the bowl. The
dry squares of food held no appeal at all.

He sighed and shook his head. There was no way he could eat this stuff.

"Good night, guys," the man said as he wheeled the cart back through the open door. He was back to reading his book.

About a minute later he returned and said, "Whoops." He shut the door

"Hey," Salem called to the raccoon. "Why aren't you eating?"

"Oh, I just don't each much these days. I'm pretty sad, being cooped up here," the raccoon answered, wiping his face with his hands.

"Humph." Salem sighed. *I wish I could get his food.* He was very hungry. He looked at Antonio and said, "How can you eat that stuff?"

"It's a challenge," Antonio answered honestly. "But you should try to eat. You'll need your strength."

"No way," Salem said. "I'll just starve myself and then they'll have to let me go."

Hey! That's it!

He raised himself up. "Like generations of prisoners before me, I'm protesting these conditions. I'm on a hunger strike!"

45

Chapter 6

Salem's night was lonely, sad, and uncomfortable. He was very hungry, too. He had hoped the Spellmans would come for him, but of course they didn't know where he was. If he'd had a harmonica, he would have played the jailhouse blues all night.

And played them well, too.

The next morning there was all kinds of bustling about at Salem's jail. Families arrived to look for lost pets, or to adopt an animal. Delilah the Pekingese was re-united with her people—a dad, a mom, and a little girl. She was so happy she cried out, "Hurray!"

But at a stern look from Salem, she clamped her mouth shut and jumped up and down instead.

There was a mystery to solve as well. When the morning keeper came to pick up the dinner dishes, Salem's bowl was empty! But he had not eaten a single bit of food.

Now no one will know I'm on a hunger strike, he thought unhappily. *Who ate my evidence?*

Sadly, more animals were brought in off the streets. A mink and an iguana were among the new prisoners, and they were both very downhearted.

Once all the people left, the animals started talking again.

"It's cold in here," the iguana groused.

He introduced himself as Iggy. "I guess it was foolish of me to escape from the pet shop."

"I want to go home!" the mink cried.

Everyone sighed. Everyone wanted to go home . . . or to have a home.

"I used to live with a great family," Fireplug informed the group. "But they had to move to a place where pets weren't permitted. So here I am."

"That's awful," Salem said, thinking of all the room he had to roam at the Spellman house.

"I'm a big dog, so it's harder for me to find a new home," Fireplug continued.

"Unfair," Antonio said indignantly.

"If I could just tell that nice young man to call my agent in Hollywood, I know they'd let me go," Maria Tacquito said. She fluttered her eyelashes at Salem. "Can I talk to him?"

"No," Salem said firmly. "Do not talk to the mortals! I mean, the people." He didn't think he should tell the other animals that he was actually a former warlock who could talk all the time. "They'll be so amazed that you're talking that they won't hear a thing you say."

"So we're stuck here," Iggy the iguana muttered. "Maybe forever."

The thought of no more tummy rubs or back scratches scared Salem.

"No!" Salem drew himself up. "Are you animals, or are you chickens? Listen, I used to rule this world."

Beside him, Antonio cleared his throat.

"Well, I *almost* ruled this world. I would have been really good at it, too. But let me tell you this. There's a way out of here and we're going to find it. I will lead you to freedom."

"Yes!" the animals chorused.

"And I have powerful friends who will be able to help you." Salem thought of Sabrina and her aunts. *Surely,* he thought, *with all their witchy powers, they could find good homes for my loyal followers.*

"My right-paw dog, Antonio, and I are going to break out of here as soon as we can. Who wants to join us?"

The others barked, yipped, woofed, cawed, and yowled so loudly that Howard burst into the room.

"What's going on?" he yelled, looking around.

The animals fell silent. He walked up and down the rows of cages.

"Maybe someone's hurt," he said to himself. "This little Chihuahua with the bandages, for example." He bent down and smiled at Antonio. "Don't worry, little fella. We'll take care of you."

Howard straightened, looked around, and sighed. "Sometimes I wish you guys could talk. Just so you could tell me if you need anything."

"Tuna," Salem mumbled under his breath.

"Well, I was getting your dinners ready, so I'll go finish up," Howard went on. "Maybe you're just hungry."

"For tuna," Salem whispered.

He turned and left the room, leaving the door wide open.

"Salem," Antonio said excitedly, "do you see that? Most of the time he doesn't shut the door."

"Hmm." Salem tapped his chin with his paw. "That's promising."

He looked at Fireplug. "What's out there?"

Fireplug shook his head. "I don't know."

"We do!" came a tiny voice directly behind Salem.

Salem whirled around. A semicircle of little white field mice wiggled their pink noses at him.

"Whoa-ho!" Salem said, amazed by their boldness. "What are you little guys doing in my cage?"

"There's a hole in the wall," one of the mice explained, pointing to it. Sure enough, there it was. "That's where we live. We tiptoed in so we wouldn't wake you up and ate your dog food."

Another mouse wiggled its whiskers and said, "And now we want to do something for you in return."

"You *do* know that I'm a cat, right?" Salem asked. "And that as a general rule, cats eat mice. And that I'm very, very hungry."

"You're different," the first mouse piped. "We can tell. You're special."

"Well, that's very true," Salem admitted modestly. He looked around. "In fact, I'm the fearless leader around here, and I'm going to lead these animals to freedom."

"Yay, Salem!" the other animals cried.

Now if I can only figure out how, Salem thought.

Chapter 7

Across town at the Hartbreak Hotel, Christophe the rabbit wiggled his nose. He wondered where Salem and Antonio were. *Zey were supposed to visit me yesterday*, the French rabbit thought. *But zey did not show up. Zey did not even call!*

The witch Christophe lived with had left Christophe alone in the hotel to go visit some friends. That had been fine with Christophe at first, but now he was lonesome. He was also getting worried about his friends.

So he decided to go to Salem's house to see what was up. It was only a hop, skip, and another hop from the hotel. Christophe was soon on the porch of the Spellman home, wondering how to ring the doorbell.

Then Sabrina, the pretty young half-witch of the family, came home from school and picked him up.

"Hello, little bunny," she said.

"Hello, I am Christophe," he announced. "I am ze friend of Salem from when he tried to take over ze world."

"Oh!" Sabrina said brightly. "Then you must know where he is. He didn't come home last night, and we've been a little worried about him."

Christophe frowned in his bunny way. "Zey are not here? But zey never arrived at ze hotel!"

"Uh-oh." Sabrina frowned back in her witchy way. Christophe thought she was charming. "Come on."

She carried him into her house. "Aunt Hilda! Aunt Zelda! Emilio!" she called. "Salem and Antonio are really missing."

Quickly she and Christophe explained what was going on. Sabrina's two aunts and their visitor looked quite concerned.

"We'll have to go out and look for them," Aunt Hilda said.

"I'll get our coats," Aunt Zelda added. "And one for you, Sabrina."

Soon the five were scouring the streets of Westbridge, searching for Salem and Antonio.

"I hope nothing happened to them," Sabrina murmured anxiously.

Me, neither, Christophe thought. But to the young witch he said, "Salem was ze most excellent leader I ever followed.

Very smart. Like ze fox, that one. And he enjoyed my cooking very much." Christophe puffed out his chest. "I, too, was on ze refreshment committee."

Hilda smiled at him. "Yes, you were. He makes a mean key lime pie."

"When we find them, I shall make ze key lime pie for everyone," he promised.

"Woo-hoo," Sabrina said. But she sounded worried.

That did not cheer Christophe up at all.

Meanwhile, at the shelter, Salem was loving his role as leader of the animals. It felt just like the old days of planning battles, instead this time they were planning an escape.

"Okay," Salem said, "the mice have reported that Howard goes down the hall to the vending machines several times a night. Lucky thing."

57

He sniffed. "And while we're talking snack food, how come some people can eat anything they want and not gain an ounce? It's not fair!"

Antonio cleared his throat to remind Salem to stick to the subject.

Salem shook himself. "Okay. When Howard goes to the vending machines, he leaves the keys on the desk where he studies."

He looked at Mojo and Jojo, the twin ferret brothers. "How's the plan going?" he asked

"We've lost a little bit," Mojo announced proudly. "It's easy!"

"Easy to be squeezy!" Jojo added. He had the habit of rhyming whenever he talked.

Salem was pleased. And envious. He had told them to run around their cages more so they could lose enough weight to squeeze through the bars of their cages. He had expected it would take several days for results. Whenever he decided to lose weight, it was very difficult.

Unfair, he thought again. *But useful.*

"Okay, good," he said to them. "Soon you'll be ready for your job. Which is what?" he coached the other followers, er, animals.

"The mice will crawl up into the vending machines and make them dispense extra treats," Antonio said. "That will keep Howard down the hall for a little extra time."

"Tick-tock, tick-tock, goes the clock!" Jojo chimed.

Mojo said, "Then we'll sneak out of our cages."

"Tippy-tippy-tippy-toe! Out the doorway we will go!" Jojo rhymed.

59

Mojo continued, "And we'll grab the keys and unlock all the cages."

"Yes!" Salem cried.

"Then we'll all sneak out the door! And we'll use the keys to open the front door."

"Bye-bye-bye, gotta fly!" Jojo cried.

"And mission accomplished!" Antonio cried.

All the animals cheered.

The door burst open.

"Everything okay in here?" Howard asked anxiously. He looked at them all sitting quietly in their cages. Then he laughed. "Yeah, right, like any of you could tell me if something was going on."

"I can, I can, Mister Man!" Jojo cried, but was immediately shushed by Mojo.

"That's funny. I thought I heard someone talking. There must be someone at the front door," Howard said.

He left the room.

As usual, he forgot to close the door.

"Ferret brothers," Salem called, "can you do it? Can you get out and save your fellow animals?"

Jojo said, "Guess it's yes!"

And Mojo cried, "Yes, I can!"

With that, Mojo popped out of his cage!

61

Chapter 8

milio, Sabrina, Hilda, Zelda, and Christophe had been walking all over Westbridge, looking for Salem and his missing friend. They had discussed using a finder's spell, but agreed that it was too public to attempt one. For the time being, they would stick to regular old searching.

Emilio said, "But if we don't find Antonio soon, I want to rethink using a finder's spell."

"I agree. We all want to find our friends," Sabrina said anxiously.

"Oui," Christophe murmured. "I feel so guilty, not being with them. We were always captured as a group during the revolution."

"I'm sure they won't hold it against you," Hilda assured him. "Especially if you make the pies."

"Ah, I hope." Christophe shrugged.

"Salem!" Sabrina called, cupping her mouth with her hands.

"Salem!" Hilda and Zelda shouted at the same time. Their voices echoed off the buildings of downtown Westbridge.

Christophe was just about to yell Salem's name as loudly as he could when a man jogged past the three witches, one warlock, and one ex-warlock. Christophe didn't want the man to know he could talk, so he just wiggled his nose. He hopped along to keep up.

"Here, let me help you," Sabrina offered. She scooped Christophe up in her arms, and they walked along.

"Salem!" everybody called.

But there was no answer.

Back in the animal shelter, Mojo had managed to get out of his cage.

"Wait wait wait, I'll get out of the grate!" his brother Jojo cried, trying to squeeze through the bars the way Mojo had done. But he was not meeting with success. He was still a little too plump.

"Mojo, just go go!" Salem whispered anxiously. "Now!"

"No no!" Jojo cried. "Wait for Jojo!"

Mojo said, "Our fearless leader wants me to go now, Jojo. I'm sorry."

"So very, very so," Jojo said sadly.

With that, Mojo scampered out of the room.

"Mice, front and center," Salem ordered.

The little ring of mice took three micey steps forward and reared up on their hind legs, standing at attention.

"To the vending machines!" Salem cried, extending his paw.

"To the vending machines!" the tallest mouse shouted.

They all saluted and followed the ferret out of the room in a miniature parade.

The escape attempt had begun. Salem looked first at Antonio, then at Fireplug. He nodded to each of them, then began pacing in his cage. He was nervous and excited all at once. *If this works, soon we'll all be free!*

65

"Well, Antonio, it doesn't get much more thrilling than this," Salem said. "It's just like the old days."

Antonio sighed. "One thing would make it better. If Christophe had also been captured. Then he would be here to enjoy the glory of our mission. I hope he's not worried about us, Salem."

Salem cocked his sharp, pointed ears. "We'll have a great story to tell him, won't we?"

After a short time Mojo returned with the keys in his mouth. He put them down and began to chitter.

"The mice have done their job!" he exclaimed. "The vending machines are giving out extra cookies and crackers. Howard's making a pig of himself. Oh, excuse me, do we have any imprisoned pigs in here?"

He looked around, then sighed with relief. "No pigs. Good. Anyway. Here are the keys!"

"Good job! Start unlocking," Salem ordered. "Anyone in here have use of their thumbs? No? Too bad."

Mojo skittered over to his brother's cage and worked to put the key in the lock. All the other animals held their breath.

This had better work, Salem thought.

"What if it doesn't work, Salem?" Antonio whispered.

"Then we move to Plan B," Salem informed him.

The little dog nodded. Then he said, "What is Plan B?"

"I have no idea," Salem confessed quietly.

"Hurry, awwooo!" Fireplug urged, pacing.

"Hurry, awwooo! Hurry, awwooo!" the parrot chittered.

Mojo tried again. And again. Salem's heart began to sink.

Then Jojo's cage swung open, and the little ferret bounded out.

"Free!" he shouted. "Me! Free! Yippee!"

The animals cheered.

"*Ssh, ssh,*" Salem urged. "Stay calm, people. Er, animals."

Suddenly there were loud footsteps on the floor.

"Quick! Back in your cages!" Salem told the ferret brothers. "Hide the keys."

"What's all this noise?" Howard demanded, walking through the door. He looked suspiciously at all the animals. "You've been so noisy lately. Ever since those two showed up."

He pointed at Salem and Antonio,

who stared at him as if they didn't understand a single word.

"All right. Everyone calm down, okay?" Howard urged.

Then he left the room and shut the door. Then there was a click and Salem realized Howard had locked it from the outside.

"Oh, no!" Maria Tacquito cried. "Now we'll never get out of here."

Salem sighed. He leaned his head sadly against his cage. Then his eyes went wide.

On the opposite side of the room was another door. But this one was latched shut on the inside. *A closet? A hallway?* Salem wondered excitedly. *Where does it go?*

His brain went into high gear. He started looking over his animals. Slowly he nodded. *With a bucket, maybe that old phone directory . . . it might work.*

69

"Okay, fellow inmates we move to Plan B!" he cried.

Antonio said quietly, "But we don't have a Plan B."

"We do now!" Salem crowed.

Chapter 9

In the animal shelter Mojo finally got all the cages unlocked. All the animals did a silent happy-feet dance, then turned to Salem for further orders.

Salem jumped up on an overturned plastic bucket and said, "This is Plan B." He waved a paw at the back door.

"See that latch? I'm going to unlatch it. We'll go out that door to freedom!" *I hope!* he added silently.

"But you're too short," Fireplug pointed out. "We're all too short."

"That's why we're going to work together to get taller," Salem said mysteriously.

Salem told everyone what to do. The ferrets used their noses to nudge the thick Westbridge phone book toward the latched door. Then Fireplug picked up the bucket in his mouth and put it on top of the phone book. Antonio found a sponge. Maria Tacquito found a scrub brush. The little mink added a discarded paper towel dispenser. The raccoon thought for a while, then added a large apple he'd been saving for a rainy day.

They made a huge pile out of all the objects.

"This is not going to stay," Salem said, walking around the tower of objects.

"Wait!"

With his teeth, Antonio unwound the bandage on his leg. The two ferrets, the raccoon, and the mink set about tying everything into a large bundle with the bandage.

"Good thinking, Antonio. *Muy bueno*," Salem said approvingly.

Maria Tacquito beamed with pride at Antonio.

"Okay, Fireplug, put your hind legs on the pile." Salem announced. "Now, Iggy, crawl on his back."

"Careful with those claws," Fireplug said anxiously.

"Never fear," Iggy told him. "They gave me a manicure at the pet shop."

"Okay, now I'll climb up on you," Salem said.

Huffing and puffing, he climbed up Fireplug's hindquarters. Then he stopped for a breath. Then he worked his way on top of Iggy and balanced himself on the iguana's head.

73

His paw almost touched the latch.

"Just a little more," he muttered, stretching up. "Hold on, everybody."

"My legs are getting tired," Fireplug announced.

"The pile is shaking," Antonio said. "Hurry, Salem."

Suddenly there was the sound of the other door opening!

"Time for dinner," Howard sang out.

Oh, no! Salem thought. *We forgot he'd be back for dinner!*

Dinner. Food. Think fast, Saberhagen. You've got followers to save!

Then he remembered Antonio's story about Hans and Fritz and the free cookies. *No one can resist free food.*

Salem scampered over to the air vent. He cleared his throat and yelled into the vent, as loudly as he could, "Pizza delivery. Did someone at the animal shelter order a pizza?" Salem hoped Howard would think someone was in the lobby and turn back.

"What?" Howard called down the hall. "I didn't order a pizza."

The key jangled in the lock! Everyone froze.

Salem yelled, "It says, Westbridge Jail. I mean, Animal Shelter."

The door stopped opening.

On the corner around from the Westbridge Animal Shelter, Sabrina froze. She said, "Isn't that Salem's voice?"

The five walked closer to an outside vent and listened.

"It is!" Christophe cried.

Sabrina frowned and asked, "What's he talking about pizza for?"

"I'll go see. Let me down," Christophe urged.

75

He scampered across the grass and peered into something that looked very like a mouse hole in the wall. Then he scampered back.

"Come on! There's no time to explain!" he cried. "Go to the front door and tell the man inside you have a pizza for him. Go go!"

The witches and Emilio gazed at one another, then did as Christophe said.

Hilda rang the doorbell and said, "Hello? We're the pizza delivery . . . um, folks."

The door burst open. A busy-looking young man frowned at them and said, "I just told you, I didn't order a pizza!"

Then he looked confused and said, "Where is it?"

"Oh." Sabrina smiled nervously, turned around so he wouldn't see her, and pointed a pizza into existence. "Here it is! Our most special pizza!"

Emilio opened the box with a grand gesture. "Does it not look *delicioso?*" he asked.

The man blinked. "Are those fish heads?" he asked.

"Oops." *And dried squids!* Without thinking, Sabrina had conjured up Salem's favorite kind of pizza.

"It's a promotion," Sabrina said brightly. "Brand-new recipe!"

Howard frowned at her. "Is this some kind of practical joke?"

Sabrina muttered to Christophe, "Now what?"

Christophe just wiggled his bunny nose and shrugged his bunny shoulders.

Salem bit the end of his pink tongue as he gave the latch one more swat.

77

It opened! And it was the back door.

"Freedom!" Salem cheered.

And then he tumbled off Iggy's head. And Iggy tumbled off Fireplug's back. And Fireplug tumbled off the bucket. And the bucket, the sponge, the scrub brush, the paper towel dispenser, and the apple went flying, making a horrible noise.

"Forward! Move, move, move!" Salem shouted to the others. They flew through the open door into the great outdoors—all except Jojo, who got confused and went the other way.

"Whoa, Jojo, whoa, whoa!" he squeaked, racing into the lobby. "Off I go, go, go!"

"Stop that ferret!" Howard shouted to Sabrina as Jojo raced between his legs. "That *talking* ferret!"

"Huh?" Sabrina asked. On the porch, she was still holding the pizza box. Then she saw the ferret, who squeaked, "Uh-oh, Jojo! I yelp! I yelp! I yelp for help!"

"Oops!" Sabrina pretended to drop the pizza box. As it fell to the floor, Jojo scooted around behind it and smacked into her ankle. Sabrina dropped to her knees, pointed her finger at the little animal, and *poof!* the animal was hidden safely inside her coat.

"I'm sorry," Sabrina said, pretending to look for the ferret. "I guess he got away."

"Oh, great!" Howard cried. He turned and ran back into the shelter. Sabrina and the others followed him.

They all skidded to a stop inside a spotless room filled with animal cages. Empty animal cages. Howard threw up his hands. "They've all escaped!"

"Woo-hoo," Sabrina whispered happily. Though she felt badly for the young man, she added, "Gotta go."

Salem was waiting for her and the others around the corner. He was surrounded by animals of all shapes and sizes, including a parrot who shouted, "Pizza! Pizza!"

"Antonio, you're safe!" Emilio said happily, picking up the Chihuahua. He gently touched the scrape on Antonio's leg. "But what's this, *amigo?* You're hurt!"

"He was wounded in the line of duty," Salem proclaimed. "He'll be getting a medal at the reunion."

"Salem, you're the one who should get a medal," Antonio said.

"He's a real hero!" Mojo added.

Jojo popped his head out of Sabrina's pocket. "Hip-hip-hurray! Salem saved the day!"

All the animals chorused their enthusiastic agreement.

Salem threw out his chest. "As usual," he said—oh, so modestly.

Epilogue

It was the big night. The Thwarted World Leaders Reunion was in full swing, complete with a band called Jewel's Collars and an all-you-can-gobble, munch, chew, or snag-with-your-tongue nacho bar.

Salem, Christophe, Antonio, and Sabrina sat at a table with a red checkered cloth, sipping root beer. Salem wore a little French beret. Antonio sported a brand-new medal, which Sabrina had pointed up for the occasion. It was adorned with Salem's mighty house cat profile, a stirring reminder of courage and daring.

"So there I was, helping my troops escape," Salem said. "Balanced on the head of Iggy the iguana. Then I fell, and things looked pret-ty bad." He smiled at Antonio and Christophe. "But by gum, we did it."

"You're the hero of the hour," Sabrina said happily. "Emilio took the talking spell off the animals. Plus, we've managed to reunite almost all the lost animals with their owners. So Howard's not in any trouble."

"Zat is wonderful!" Christophe said.

Sabrina continued, "And we're finding homes for the strays. We've already taken Fireplug to live with a really nice family."

Antonio grinned as Maria Tacquito turned and waved at him. "And I'm getting married!" he announced happily. "To a TV star! Emilio is going to help her get her career back on track. We're moving to Hollywood!"

Salem threw back his head and laughed.

Antonio was right, he thought. *This is all going to make a great story for our memoirs!*

I can't wait for next year's reunion! I'm sure we'll have even more amazing adventures to share!

Cat Care Tips

#1 You should *never* hit a cat to discipline it. They will respond just as well to a loud voice or other noise (such as the rattle of a can with some coins in it), a squirt of water, or a gentle push.

#2 If you are having problems with certain unwanted behaviors with your cats (such as jumping on counters, fighting with other cats, urinating around the house, etc.), you should seek the advice of an expert (a veterinarian or a trainer/behaviorist).

#3 Forceful and aggressive discipline is very hard on cats and rarely works.

—Laura E. Smiley, MS, DVM, Dipl. ACVIM
Gwynedd Veterinary Hospital

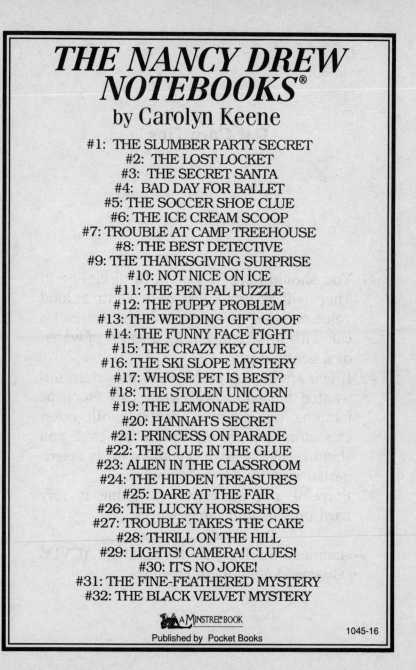

THE NANCY DREW NOTEBOOKS®
by Carolyn Keene

#1: THE SLUMBER PARTY SECRET
#2: THE LOST LOCKET
#3: THE SECRET SANTA
#4: BAD DAY FOR BALLET
#5: THE SOCCER SHOE CLUE
#6: THE ICE CREAM SCOOP
#7: TROUBLE AT CAMP TREEHOUSE
#8: THE BEST DETECTIVE
#9: THE THANKSGIVING SURPRISE
#10: NOT NICE ON ICE
#11: THE PEN PAL PUZZLE
#12: THE PUPPY PROBLEM
#13: THE WEDDING GIFT GOOF
#14: THE FUNNY FACE FIGHT
#15: THE CRAZY KEY CLUE
#16: THE SKI SLOPE MYSTERY
#17: WHOSE PET IS BEST?
#18: THE STOLEN UNICORN
#19: THE LEMONADE RAID
#20: HANNAH'S SECRET
#21: PRINCESS ON PARADE
#22: THE CLUE IN THE GLUE
#23: ALIEN IN THE CLASSROOM
#24: THE HIDDEN TREASURES
#25: DARE AT THE FAIR
#26: THE LUCKY HORSESHOES
#27: TROUBLE TAKES THE CAKE
#28: THRILL ON THE HILL
#29: LIGHTS! CAMERA! CLUES!
#30: IT'S NO JOKE!
#31: THE FINE-FEATHERED MYSTERY
#32: THE BLACK VELVET MYSTERY

A MINSTREL® BOOK
Published by Pocket Books

1045-16

The Hardy Boys® are:

THE CLUES BROTHERS™

#1 The Gross Ghost Mystery

#2 The Karate Clue

#3 First Day, Worst Day

#4 Jump Shot Detectives

#5 Dinosaur Disaster

#6 Who Took the Book?

#7 The Abracadabra Case

#8 The Doggone Detectives

#9 The Pumped-Up Pizza Problem

#10 The Walking Snowman

#11 The Monster in the Lake

#12 King for a Day

#13 Pirates Ahoy!

#14 All Eyes on First Prize

By Franklin W. Dixon

Look for a brand-new story every other month

A MINSTREL® BOOK

Published by Pocket Books

1398-09

What's it like to be a witch?

Sabrina
The Teenage Witch™

"I'm 16, I'm a witch, and I still have to go to school?"

♦♦♦♦♦♦♦♦

#1 Sabrina, the Teenage Witch
#2 Showdown at the Mall
#3 Good Switch, Bad Switch
#4 Halloween Havoc
#5 Santa's Little Helper
#6 Ben There, Done That
#7 All You Need Is A Love Spell
#8 Salem on Trial
#9 A Dog's Life
#10 Losta Luck
#11 Prisoner of Cabin 13
#12 All That Glitters
#13 Go Fetch
#14 Spying Eyes
Sabrina Goes to Rome
#15 Harvest Moon
#16 Now You See Her, Now You Don't
#17 Eight Spells a Week
#18 I'll Zap Manhattan
#19 Shamrock Shenanigans
#20 Age of Aquariums
#21 Prom Time
#22 Witchopoly
#23 Bridal Bedlam
#24 Scarabian Nights
#25 While the Cat's Away
#26 Fortune Cookie Fox

Based on the hit ABC-TV series

From Archway Paperbacks
Published by Pocket Books

1346-06